For Amy and Alicia
~ M. S.
For Kin and Tridge
~ L. F.

tiger tales

5 River Road, Suite 128, Wilton, CT 06897

Published in the United States 2019

Originally published in Great Britain 2019

by Little Tiger Press Ltd.

Text copyright © 2019 Mark Sperring

Illustrations copyright © 2019 Lucy Fleming

ISBN-13: 978-1-68010-173-7

ISBN-10: 1-68010-173-0

Printed in China

LTP/1400/2645/0219

For more insight and activities, visit us at www.tigertalesbooks.com

THE MOST WONDERFUL GIFT in the WORLD

by Mark Sperring

Illustrated by Lucy Fleming

tiger tales

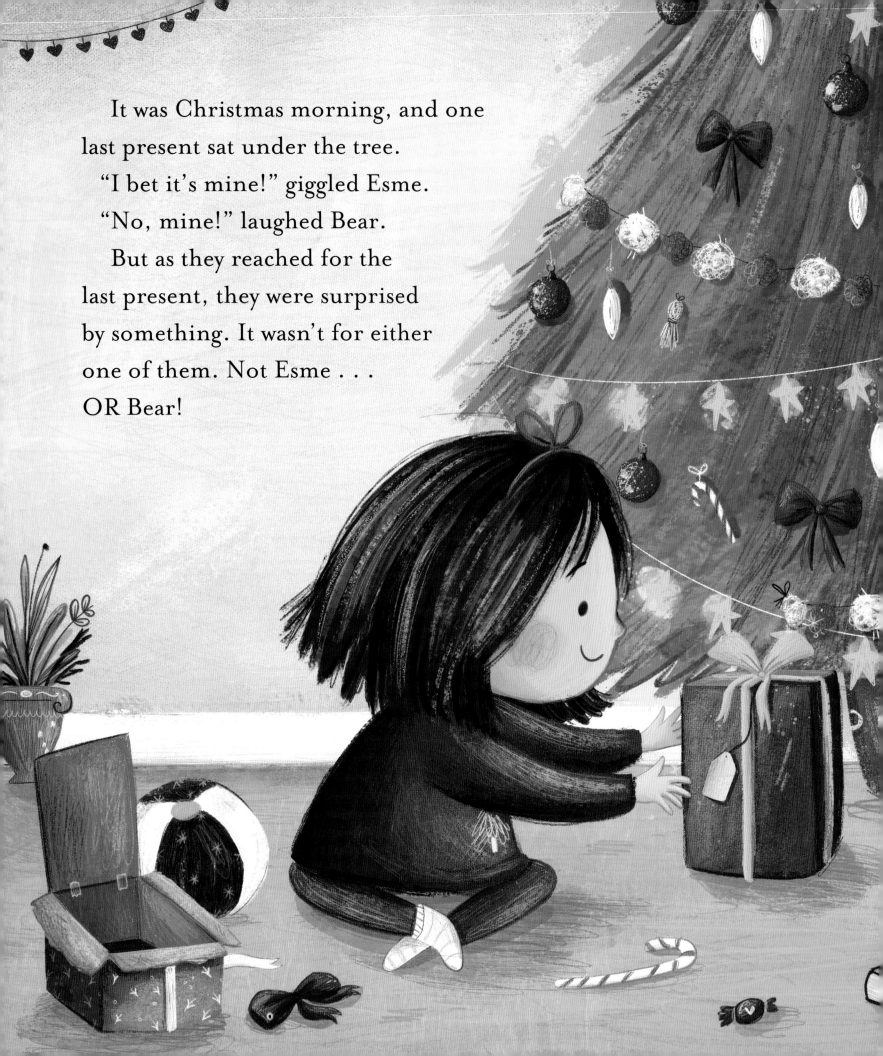

It was Christmas morning, and one last present sat under the tree.

"I bet it's mine!" giggled Esme.

"No, mine!" laughed Bear.

But as they reached for the last present, they were surprised by something. It wasn't for either one of them. Not Esme . . . OR Bear!

The tag read *For Little Bunny Boo-Boo, Love Santa.*
"Well," said Esme, "in all the busy
JuMbLE - TuMbleNesS of Christmas, somebody's present
has been mixed up with ours."
BUT WHAT SHOULD THEY DO?

"Let's open it!" said Bear, giving it a BEARISH sniff.
Esme had a better idea. "Let's find Little Bunny Boo-Boo
and make sure she gets her gift!"

So they put on their
warm winter clothes and
set out into the snow.

They had not gone far when they came across a sign.

FOR LITTLE BUNNY BOO-BOO'S HOUSE, FOLLOW THE **TREACHEROUS PATH**

"The TREACHEROUS path!" gulped Bear. "I don't like the sound of that!"
"How TREACHEROUS can it be?" shrugged Esme, sure they'd both be fine.

But OH, DEAR! The path was VERY treacherous indeed!

With SLIPPY parts . . .

and SLIDEY parts . . .

... and FALL-DOWN-ON-YOUR-BOTTOM parts!

BUMP!

After much slip-sliding around,
they came across another sign.

FOR LITTLE BUNNY BOO-BOO'S
HOUSE, WALK THROUGH THE
**HOWLING
GALE!**

Bear looked worried, but Esme gave him a comforting pat.

"How HOWLY can a gale be?" she said.

But suddenly, the wind picked up and
blasted them right in the face . . .

Wooooooooo!

Wooooooooo!

"Can't we just keep Little Bunny Boo-Boo's present and go back home?" begged Bear.
"Of course not!" called Esme over the GROWLING-HOWLING GALE.

Soon the wind died down,
and they came to the last sign.

Little Bunny Boo-Boo's
house is just beyond the
DEEP, DEEP snow drifts.
WARNING: THEY REALLY
ARE **DEEP!**

When the snow reached Esme's knees,
Bear scooped her high up onto his shoulders
and carried her for the rest of the way.
"Straight ahead for Little Bunny Boo-Boo's
house!" cheered Esme as a snow-covered
cabin came into view.

When they got there,
they could not have been happier.
First, Little Bunny Boo-Boo
was so happy to see them.

Second, it was COZY-WARM!
And third, when they looked around,
they saw that Little Bunny Boo-Boo
had not received ONE SINGLE
Christmas present. Poor thing!

So Bear handed the gift to her, and they all
huddled together to see what was inside.

"Maybe it's a game!" smiled Esme.

"Or peppermints!" beamed Bear.

BUT imagine Esme and Bear's surprise when
Little Bunny Boo-Boo opened the gift and it was
ABSOLUTELY EMPTY with
NOTHING INSIDE AT ALL . . .

. . . except for a teeny-tiny handwritten note,
on the smallest scrap of paper.

Dear Little Bunny Boo-Boo,
Here is exactly what
you asked for!

Love, Santa

Little Bunny Boo-Boo stared at Esme and
Bear, and her eyes grew wide with joy.
"I've just moved into my little cabin," she said,
"and I haven't had time to make a single friend.
So, this year, I asked Santa for a VERY special gift . . . ."

"A friend (maybe even two) who was honest and true, who would walk a TREACHEROUS PATH, battle the HOWLIEST of GALES, and brave the DEEPEST OF SNOW DRIFTS to stand by my side."

"So you see," smiled
Little Bunny Boo-Boo, "Santa's
present to me . . . IS YOU!"

"US?" asked Esme and Bear,
thinking that maybe a jump rope
or blocks might have been better!

But after they'd enjoyed a Christmas Day
full of laughter and many delicious things
to eat, they all agreed that things like jump ropes
and blocks were very nice, but . . .
a TRUE friend (maybe even two) was the
BEST and MOST WONDERFUL gift of all!